# Crash

## Lesley Choyce

*Orca soundings*

ORCA BOOK PUBLISHERS

**Library and Archives Canada Cataloguing in Publication**

Choyce, Lesley, 1951-
Crash / Lesley Choyce.
(Orca soundings)

Issued also in electronic format.
ISBN 978-1-4598-0525-5 (bound).--ISBN 978-1-4598-0522-4 (pbk.)

I. Title.  II. Series: Orca soundings
PS8555.H668C73 2013       jc813'.54       C2013-901923-5

First published in the United States, 2013
**Library of Congress Control Number:** 2013935382

**Summary:** Cameron thinks he can survive anything on willpower alone.
Not this time.

MIX
Paper from
responsible sources
FSC® C016245

*Orca Book Publishers is dedicated to preserving the environment and has
printed this book on Forest Stewardship Council® certified paper.*

Orca Book Publishers gratefully acknowledges the support for its publishing
programs provided by the following agencies: the Government of Canada through
the Canada Book Fund and the Canada Council for the Arts,
and the Province of British Columbia through the BC Arts Council
and the Book Publishing Tax Credit.

Cover image by Getty Images

ORCA BOOK PUBLISHERS
PO Box 5626, Stn. B
Victoria, BC Canada
V8R 6S4

ORCA BOOK PUBLISHERS
PO Box 468
Custer, WA USA
98240-0468

www.orcabook.com
Printed and bound in Canada.

16  15  14  13  •  4  3  2  1

## Chapter One

It just hit me. I was at the New Year's Eve party at Brian's house. At first my plan was to get loaded. The usual. It had been quite the year. Busted for stealing a car, almost caught making a drug delivery for a dealer, and maybe a few more bad moves on my part. I guess I hadn't found my focus yet, my path.

I liked living on the edge a bit, and one thing kept leading to another.

But there I was at Brian's, feeling oddly out of place, watching everyone else having a good time.

And suddenly it felt all wrong.

I turned sixteen three days ago. Nobody likes having a birthday right after Christmas, but then, this Christmas had not been anything special. Some kind of new weirdness going on between my mom and dad, and things had been a bit tense ever since my dad lost his job. It seemed like no one cared about my birthday. Me included. I found myself staring into the mirror, wondering who was looking back at me. After that I just had this weird feeling in my gut. I felt unsettled. I was about to freak, I thought. I was about to do something really stupid.

And New Year's Eve at Brian's was probably where it would happen.

But instead of me freaking out, something different happened.

I had only had one beer. Everyone else was way ahead of me. They were all laughing and having a great time. But I set the beer down and took a deep breath.

And suddenly everything became clear.

I knew who that person in the mirror was. It was the old me. And the old me wasn't what I wanted. I swear I'd never made a New Year's resolution in my life. I just knew that this was the year I was going to turn it around. I was going to get my shit together. No more messing around. No more talking. No more lies. No, this was not one of those half-assed New Year's resolutions. This was the real thing.

I suddenly felt clear-headed and weirdly happy.

So I walked out of there and down the dark, cold street, sucking in sweet, clean winter air. I don't think anyone even noticed me leaving.

When I got home, no one was there. No one but my dog, Ozzie. Part Lab and part German shepherd, Ozzie was a good old dog. Always happy to see me. Always there for me. I tucked into bed with Ozzie sleeping beside me on the floor.

I fell asleep focused on a new beginning.

## Chapter Two

I had a good night's sleep, but nothing could have prepared me for what came next. I think it was about eight o'clock when my dad knocked on my door.

"Come on in," I said.

He walked in and sat down on the side of my bed. He looked like something was bugging him. I thought maybe I was about to get a lecture for something

I had done, so I decided to tell him about the night before. "I have some stuff I want to share with you," I said.

He held up his hand. "Not now, Cameron. I've got some of my own stuff I've got to tell you." Man, he looked serious. I was thinking, Oh shit, what's this about?

He couldn't look me in the eye. He just bent down and started petting Ozzie. "Cameron, you know things haven't been so good around here with me out of work. And your mother and I have been having our problems."

I was feeling a little scared then. "Yeah, well, so that's nothing new. Things will smooth out."

He shook his head. "No, they won't. I'm going crazy around here. I've decided I'm going to head out west and get work. It's what I have to do."

I felt like someone had smacked me in the face. "When are you going?"

"Today," he said. "Now."

"Dad, you can't just do that."

"I'm sorry, Cam. I'll call you from out west." He stood up, leaned over me and gave me a hug like he used to when I was a little kid. And then he left my room. Ozzie knew something was wrong, and he hopped up onto my bed.

I heard the front door open and close, and then I heard the car start. And then, I guess, he was gone.

I don't know how long I lay there in shock, thinking this was something that happened to other kids but not to me. If I had known what was coming next, I don't think I would have gotten out of bed that day.

But eventually I did.

Downstairs, my mom was sitting at the kitchen table with a cup of coffee in her hand.

"Cameron, we need to talk," she said.

I let Ozzie outside and then sat down across from her. I suddenly had a flashback to the party the night before, and I was thinking now that maybe I should have stayed and gotten really wasted. "Dad's gone. I know," I said.

She nodded. "It's my fault," she said.

"What do you mean? I know things have been tough since he lost his job."

"It's not just that."

"Then what?"

"Things haven't been the same in the last year. And I'm sorry, but I haven't been exactly honest with you. I've been seeing someone else."

"*What?* Who?" I couldn't believe my mother was saying this.

She took a sip of her coffee. "Nick."

That was my second slap in the face that morning. "Nick? Nick's an asshole." Nick was my father's friend. I'd always thought he was one of the biggest bullshitters I'd ever met. This couldn't be real.

"I'm sorry. It just happened. I didn't mean for things to go this way."

Ozzie was scratching at the door, and I got up to let him in.

"I think Nick is the real thing," she continued. "I think this is finally my chance to be happy."

I wanted to scream out every obscene word I could think of, but my brain grabbed on to that odd word— *happy*. Wasn't that what my revelation was about last night? I was going to clean up my act and learn how to be happy? And now this crap.

"Now that your father's gone…"

I cut her off. "Is that why he left? Because of you and Asshole Nick?"

She didn't answer me. "Now that your father's gone, I won't be able to keep up the rent on this house. Besides, there are too many memories here. I need a new start. We need to go someplace else."

"Where?"

She couldn't look at me. "Nick says he wants me to move in with him. You can come too, of course."

I shook my head. "This is insane."

"No, Nick said you could have the whole basement to yourself."

The nightmare continued. I looked down at Oz. He gave me his paw. I knew I couldn't move in with Nick, and then I remembered something else. "Nick hates dogs."

My mom shrugged. "Yeah. I guess we'll have to find another home for Ozzie. We can work this out." And then, more confidently, she said, "We can make this work. I know we can."

"This is all bull," I said. I grabbed my coat and walked out into the cold, bright day with Ozzie trailing behind me.

"Welcome to the new year," I said to no one as I walked out to the street, my breath puffing small angry clouds into the morning air.

## Chapter Three

It was one of those nasty cold winter mornings. The sun was out, but it was way below freezing. Ozzie was happy to be tagging along, sniffing at every tree and post and peeing on everything he sniffed. I didn't need to keep Oz on a leash. He was well trained. He was a good dog. And I wasn't going to give him up.

I wasn't dressed warmly enough, but I didn't want to go back into the house to get gloves or a heavier coat. I cursed my cheating mother and my runaway father. I didn't know who to blame most. I thought maybe my mom. She and stupid-ass Nick. Maybe that was really why my father had left.

I thought about my decision the night before to clean up my act. That lightning bolt from out of nowhere. Who was I kidding? Right now if someone were to offer me a drink or a toke, I'd gladly take them up on it. Forget about getting clean. Just stay stoned.

We were in the park now, and the voices inside my head were still screaming. This just couldn't be happening to me. At first I thought the park was empty. The whole town was probably at home nursing hangovers. Everyone but me. Then Ozzie spotted something tucked between two bushes, and he loped over to check it out. I followed him.

It was a pup tent dusted lightly with snow from the previous night. A pup tent? Who the hell would be camping out here in the middle of winter? Something moved inside. Ozzie barked. And he usually wasn't much of a barker.

From inside a girl's voice said, "Leave me alone."

Ozzie barked more loudly, but I muzzled him with my chilly hands. "Be good."

I watched as the zipper on the tent slowly opened. A hand popped out first and then a head. Long straggly hair and the frightened face of girl. Real frightened. "Leave me alone," she repeated. She looked at me and then stared at Ozzie.

"Ozzie won't hurt you," I said. But she wasn't convinced. She popped back into the tent. Then she unzipped it all the way and jumped out. She was wearing a man's winter coat. Whoever this girl was, I was thinking, she must be crazy. Maybe totally flipped out on drugs. She turned her back to me and started to hastily knock down the tent.

"Just stay back," she said, brushing the snow off the flimsy tent. She stuffed it into one of those big rolling suitcases.

"Hey, I'm sorry," I said. "Look, I'm not the police or anything. I didn't mean to disturb you. I was just out walking. Ozzie got curious."

The whole tent was in her suitcase. Like she'd done this manic breaking camp before. "What are you doing sleeping out here, anyway?" I asked.

She looked me in the eye for the first time. I could still read the fear. But I couldn't help noticing her green eyes. How pretty they were. "It was just a dare," she said. "I was just camping."

"Wow," I said. "I guess you won that bet."

She started to walk away, towing that suitcase behind her. "Wait," I said, following her. I really wanted the whole story. I wanted to know about the girl who camped out in January in the freezing cold, all alone.

"Leave me alone," she said. And there was no denying that she meant it. You could tell she'd said it to others many times before.

For some reason, I felt like I needed to talk to this weird, crazy girl more than anything else on this crazy first day of the year. I tapped Ozzie. He understood. He pranced toward the girl and nuzzled her hand. At first she waved him off, but then he did it a second time. She petted him this time but still kept walking. I was following behind, and I watched as Ozzie gently bumped into her with his nose.

The girl stopped. She petted him. I hung back for a second. Then I cleared my throat and spoke. "It's friggin' cold out here. I don't live far away. Why don't you come back with me and warm up for a bit?"

She continued to pet Ozzie but didn't look up.

"I'll cook you breakfast," I said. "I suck at cooking, but I can do eggs."

She shook her head.

"Hey," I said. "I don't know who you are, but you look really cold. I'm freezing my ass here too, and I don't even want to go home. You wanna hear about my morning? I wake up, and my father says he's moving away to find work. Then my mom tells me she's about to shack up with one of my dad's old buddies, who is a certified scumbag." I paused and took a swallow of that cold, hard air. "So do you want to walk away, or do you want to come join me in my nightmare?"

I guess it was the way I delivered that last line that brought her around. She looked at me with those green eyes again. And she let slip a hint of a smile.

## Chapter Four

I didn't know what I was going to say to my mom. But I really didn't care what she thought. We walked slowly against a cold north wind, Ozzie prancing beside us. I tried to help the girl with her suitcase, but she tugged it back.

My mom's car was gone. I breathed a sigh of relief. On the kitchen table was a note. *Gone to Nick's. Will call you later.*

*Everything will work out okay. I promise. Love, Mom.* I showed it to the girl. She read it, and I saw a look of sadness come over her face. Then I crumpled up the note and threw it across the room.

"I'm Cameron," I said. "You've already met Ozzie. Welcome to my humble abode." I don't know where that line came from.

She pulled her hood down. "I'm Mackenzie. Some people call me Mac." The name Mac didn't fit her at all. Her cheeks were red from the cold. Mine probably were too. Her hair was long and tangled. I was beginning to think it wasn't just her eyes that were pretty. The girl was cute. She took off the big winter coat, and I saw she had another jacket and a hoodie on under it. It was definitely the layered look. "Got any coffee?" she blurted out suddenly.

I laughed. "Sure." I boiled some water and made her a cup of instant coffee.

She watched intently but didn't say a word. Then she seemed to relax. And suddenly the world didn't seem to be such a hateful place.

I tried asking her about herself but mostly got one-word answers. It was clear that she'd had a rough life. She didn't come out and say it, but I was getting the feeling that she was on her own. Really on her own. I scrambled some eggs, burned some toast and made more coffee. She ate like a horse and drank three cups of coffee.

I could tell she was happy to be inside and warm, and I tried to make her feel at home. After she'd finished eating, she fed some scraps of toast and bits of egg to Ozzie and then just sat with him on the kitchen floor. I'd often said Ozzie was a bit of a babe magnet, but this was different. I really didn't know what to make of her. But then, my life was down the toilet, so all I could think was that it was great to have some company.

Sometime around noon, I heard a vehicle pull up. It was Nick's big-ass truck. Mackenzie stood up as if she was about to run, but I told her to stay put.

You can picture the scene. Mom and Nick walked in, saw the girl with the long tangled hair. Ozzie growled at Nick. Mom growled at me.

Against my protests, Mackenzie slowly put on her coats and inched her suitcase toward the door while Nick stared at her like he was looking at a criminal. My mom was going off on a tirade about not being able to "trust" me, which seemed kind of screwy, considering what she had been up to. I told her so. Nick tried to wade into it, and I told him to shut up.

"I'll just wait outside," Mac said politely.

"Don't go anywhere," I said. "Please."

She smiled. "I won't," she said. I could understand why she didn't want to be part of our family dispute, and it was just as well that she left, because I started sharing my disrespectful thoughts about Nick and my mom. It was not the most polite conversation. It was clear that my mom had come back for some of her things and was going to be staying with Nick.

"Cameron," Nick said, trying to contain himself. "If you're going to be living at my house, you'll have to be more respectful to your mother."

It wasn't exactly a warm invitation. And it wasn't anything I wanted to hear, anyway. "Bite me," I told him in a cool, level voice.

And then it was over. My mom was crying, and Nick was trying to hold his temper, and then they were back in his truck and driving off.

When I went outside to get Mackenzie, she was nowhere to be found. I had no idea where to find her, and I felt more alone than ever.

I went back in and sat on the kitchen floor where Mackenzie had been sitting. I leaned over and hugged Ozzie. Then I fell into some kind of black hole. I didn't see anything in the days ahead worth living for. Living with Nick? No way. Going back to school? Bleak and boring. I guess I sat there on the floor for a long time. And then I was pissed off at myself. Mostly for letting the girl walk out of my house and losing her.

"Let's go find her," I said to Ozzie.

Now, it's not like Ozzie is some great tracking dog or anything. He's just a dog who understands my feelings, and he knew what needed to be done. So we went for a walk. I was really bundled up this time, ready for the worst, and I had Ozzie's leash. I didn't know how far we might have to go. I mean, how far could a girl roll a big suitcase in a city full of snow?

The answer to that question was "far." I don't know how we did it, but finally, after me following as Ozzie led, there she was, sitting in a rundown coffee shop downtown. I took a chance and went in with the dog. I got looks, but no one said anything. Mackenzie was asleep at one of the tables, and Ozzie nudged her awake.

"How'd you find me?"

I pointed to Oz. "He likes you," I said. What I wanted to say was that I liked her. I needed a friend. And I was getting the picture. I guess I'd had it from the start. Mackenzie was no extreme-sport teenage winter camper. "You look tired," I said.

"I am tired."

"Things didn't go so well with Mom and her boyfriend."

"Been there. Done that," she said. "You weren't kidding when you invited me into your nightmare."

"Well, yeah. I guess you got the picture that we aren't one big happy family. Too bad my dad wasn't there to express his thoughts about Nick and Mom."

"Adults have their problems."

"So I've noticed. But here's the thing. My mom wants to stay with Nick. Nick doesn't really want me around. And he wants nothing to do with Ozzie. In fact, Mom wants me to give Ozzie away."

"What are you going to do?"

"I'm not giving Ozzie away."

Mackenzie gave me the soft smile I'd seen only once before. "Good for you."

"But what I'm leading up to is this. You need a place to stay. I'm freaking out there, being by myself with all the weird stuff happening in my life." I took a deep gulp. "So come stay with me."

I don't think she saw this coming. Hell, I didn't see it coming. The words just kind of leaped out. She sat there in silent shock. I kept talking. "My dad is gone, and I'm not going to let Mom or Nick run my life. I'm sixteen, and they dumped all this crap on me. Wasn't my fault. So as far as I see it, I'm on my own. And none of them are going to boot me out of my own house."

"But who owns the house?"

"The landlord. It's rented. But he doesn't know what's going on. So I think I'm okay there. Come stay as long as you like."

"I can't do that," she said. "I've been down this road too many times before."

"Where are you going to stay, then?"

"I've got options."

"Yeah, but they must not be great options if I found you holed up in a tent in the park for New Year's Eve."

"Like I said, it was a dare."

I smiled but didn't call her a liar. "Let's go," I said. Ozzie wagged his tail, and that seemed to do the trick.

It was dark now as we walked through the silent city. It felt like it was about to snow again. We were quiet at first. I was wondering why I was doing this. I knew nothing about this girl I'd found in a tent. Then she broke the silence.

"If I'm going to stay with you, you've got to go along with my rules."

Rules were the farthest thing from my mind. "What kind of rules?"

"My rules. Like you need to leave me alone when I need to be left alone."

"I'm okay with that."

"And just 'cause I'm in your house, it doesn't mean you own me."

I nodded. I had a good idea of what she was talking about.

"And if I go out to do some stuff on my own, you can't always be bugging me, asking questions. You can't be my father."

"Of course not."

"And you're not my boyfriend."

I shrugged.

"And we need to be kind and respectful to each other."

That one caught me off guard. I had been thinking of Mackenzie as tough and streetwise. But this was something different. "Of course," I said. "What else?"

"That's it."

We walked the rest of the way in silence. The truth was, I was more than a little scared. I had no idea what I was getting myself into. I had no idea how the next few weeks of my life were going to unfold. All I knew was that Mackenzie was walking beside me, spelling out her rules. And she was going to be staying at my house. And that I wasn't quite so alone anymore.

## Chapter Five

I settled Mackenzie into the spare bedroom and showed her around the house. "You sure it's okay for me to stay here?" she asked. I could tell she thought it was too good to be true and that she wasn't used to anyone being nice to her. The house wasn't anything special, but I guess it was a castle compared to a pup tent in the park and wherever else she'd been crashing.

"Consider this your home. You can stay here as long as I'm here. And I'm not planning on going anywhere."

She smiled a soft, sad smile and headed off to the bathroom to take a shower. An hour later, she showed up in the kitchen. I almost thought she was a different person. "You clean up real nice," I said with a fake southern accent. It was some line I'd heard in a movie.

Mackenzie blushed and said, "Thanks. I haven't felt this good in a long time."

I found a frozen pizza in the freezer and baked it for us. It wasn't very good, but she seemed to really enjoy it. I kept waiting for her to share her story, even bits of her life. But she didn't. She got uncomfortable when I asked questions.

"I have to go back to school tomorrow," I said. "Can you take care of

Ozzie while I'm gone? Let him out and keep him company?"

"Sure. For some reason I didn't think you were still in school."

"Yeah. I am. It mostly sucks. But I don't have a clue what else to do with my life."

"I dropped out last fall. I found it didn't quite fit in with my lifestyle."

I couldn't help but laugh at her putting it that way. "Your lifestyle?"

"Don't make fun of me."

"Sorry." She was sensitive. "It's got to be tough out there."

"Yeah, it is tough *out there*. I was couch surfing, crashing with some okay people and then some not-so-okay people. Showing up at school looking… well, you saw me."

I nodded. She was introducing me to a world I knew nothing about. "So you dropped out?"

"I didn't want to. Like you, I didn't have a clue what I wanted to do with my life. I guess all I really want to do right now is survive."

That shocked me, but I tried not to show it. "You mean it, don't you?"

She nodded.

I almost thought I was gonna cry. It wasn't just her, I realized, it was me too. We were different, but after what had happened earlier, I was thinking the same thing. I just wanted to get through this and be able to live my life.

Ozzie was sitting on the floor between us, and he looked up just then. "We'll help you, won't we, Oz?" I said to my dog. "We'll get through this together." And as the words slipped out of my mouth, I realized I had never made a commitment like that to anyone in my life.

School sucked. I left Mackenzie at home watching crappy morning

TV with Ozzie, and I hoofed it to high school. You could tell most teachers didn't want to be there either on that first day back after vacation. Mr. Clayton, my math teacher, and Ms. Hollis, my biology teacher, both warned me that I was on academic probation and most likely to fail their courses. They weren't offering any encouragement, just threats I didn't need to hear. I wanted to tell them both to screw off, but I kept my mouth shut. Davis Conlon, a classmate who had been ragging me since I was twelve, said he'd seen me downtown. "That was one sorry-looking homely bitch you were with," he said.

I could have taken him right there, but I was thinking about how pretty Mackenzie actually was. And she was living in my house. And I thought back to New Year's Eve and my promise to my new self. I'd already broken a couple of my own "rules," but I wouldn't let

Dickhead Davis Conlon drag me down. I gave him a hard look. "She's a friend," I said as calmly as I could. "A new friend. And we were hanging out."

"Yeah, I know about hanging out with her. I know who she is."

I didn't know what he meant, but I wasn't going to continue the conversation. The sooner I got away from him, the less likely I was to slam him into a locker.

I made it through the school day and avoided a couple more traps. I decided my New Year's decision was not such a bad one. I could pull things together at school if given a chance. I'd do it for me. And I'd do it for her.

On the walk home, I began to worry that she might not be there, that she'd have disappeared like before.

But I was wrong. She was in her room. The door was open, and she was asleep with her clothes on, curled up with Ozzie. I stood there for a minute, just watching her breathe. Ozzie didn't even get up. He looked at me and wagged his tail gently. They both looked about as contented as anything could be.

# Chapter Six

The school week ended, and I still hadn't gotten into trouble. I had barely passed a math test and squeaked through one in biology. But I was doing the work and keeping my head down. At home, Mackenzie and I were eating whatever we could find in the freezer, and I was running low on dog food.

The phone rang quite a few times, and I knew it was Mom because Nick's number came up. Maybe my dad phoned too, but I wasn't answering. Mac took Ozzie for walks while I was at school, and she started cooking dinner and making sandwiches for my lunch. Yeah, I know. We were like this little family. I learned not to ask her too much about her past, but a few things slipped out. Her mom had been hooked on crack, and she hated her father. Hated him and refused to talk about him. She'd been on her own for over a year. Social services hadn't been much help. Group homes were definitely not for her.

But we were okay. I was playing by her rules, and I was close to sticking to my own. On the weekend, we were sitting in the kitchen, talking, when my mom walked in without knocking. She looked at both of us and then straight at me. "Cameron, what are you doing? Who is this?"

"I'm not doing anything to you," I said. "I'm just trying to live my life."

Mom was holding back, trying not to explode. "You need to come live with Nick and me. And she has to go."

Mackenzie just sat there, staring at the floor.

I had a lot I wanted to say about who had screwed up everything. But I held back.

"Right now. You need to come with me."

I shook my head.

"Then we need to call your father, and you can go out there and be with him." I could tell by the way she said it that this was what she really preferred. It would solve all her worries. She'd have her little love nest with Nick, and I'd be out of the way.

"I'm not gonna do that," I said. I took a deep breath. "Look, Mom, I know what you think you see here, but it's not like that. I'm going to school, and Mackenzie needs a place to stay." Those words just didn't seem right. But I knew whatever I said, it would sound all wrong. I felt so frustrated, I almost didn't speak, but then it came out. "We're good for each other. We're both staying here. And that's final."

My mom looked like she was going to explode. Ozzie growled. Mom started banging around the place, knocking things over and grabbing stuff that was hers. She had an armful of magazines and cookbooks and some clothes when she came back into the room. She glared at me. "Cameron, I want you to get in that car now," she said in a low, mean voice.

I shook my head and didn't budge. She let out a frustrated huff and walked out the door. Mackenzie and I tried to pretend it hadn't happened, but it put a dark cloud over the rest of the day. We knew our warm little world could not last forever.

"When I moved out on my mom," she said, "I felt like I was abandoning her forever. I knew she was headed downhill, but I couldn't stop her. And I couldn't stay there and live that life anymore. But it was really scary. I stayed with friends for a while, but their parents eventually complained. Maybe you should move in with her."

"It's not an option. But tell me more about you. How did you survive on your own?"

"I had to work on it day by day. I tried a couple of shelters, but the people I met there were not good to be around. They were dragging me down, and I was better off on my own." She saw the worry in my face, I guess.

"Look," she said. "I know I can't stay here forever. This is great. But it's not gonna last. Maybe I should move on before things start to get ugly."

I didn't want to lose her. I swallowed hard. "Whatever happens, let's face it together, Mac. You're, like, the best thing that has happened to me in a long time. Maybe you're the best thing that's ever happened in my life."

She looked me in the eyes and leaned forward. She kissed me on the forehead. I wanted that moment to last forever.

Nick arrived the next morning when I was getting ready to go to school. Ozzie was still in the bedroom with Mac, so he wasn't around to growl. Nick had his speech well rehearsed, and he was playing Mr. Rational. "Look, Cameron, I understand how you feel about me and your mom, and you have a right to that. But she's really upset, and I'm wondering if we can sort this out. Me and you."

"I don't know, Nick. What do you want me to do?"

"Move in with us. You'll have the basement. You won't hardly ever have to deal with me. It'll be like having your own apartment."

I wouldn't do that in a million years. But I thought I'd play the game. "What about Ozzie? Can he come too?"

Nick didn't like that, but I guess he thought he was going to be the hero peacekeeper. "Sure," he conceded. "Keep him down there. And you'll have your own entrance, so you can just take him out the back to the yard, and I think it might all work."

"What about Mackenzie? Can she come too? She needs a place to live."

I knew Nick wouldn't go for that. "No. Your mom would never allow that.

That girl's not your responsibility. I don't know her story, but that's what we have social services for. They'll take care of her."

"I'm not moving in without Mackenzie."

I guess it was noble on Nick's part to come over at all and offer what he was offering. But I knew that if I moved to his place, Ozzie would be gone in no time. And I'd be under his rule. Nick liked to have his way. This was all a ploy to keep my mom happy. Nick pounded his fist into his palm. Once. Twice. Three times. I thought the next one might be directed at me. He sucked in his breath and said, "Cameron, I've been trying to be reasonable with you. We both have. But this is bullshit."

Funny that he would use that word.

"Yeah, Nick," I said. "I figured out it was all bullshit a long time ago. So you might as well suck it up and live with it."

Nick stormed out, and the house grew quiet again. I watched him drive away in his big black truck. When I turned around, I saw Mackenzie standing there. She had heard the whole thing.

## Chapter Seven

We made it through another weekend. Mackenzie and me and Ozzie. I put Nick out of my mind. And I didn't answer the phone, even though I knew my mom and probably my dad were calling. By now we were almost out of food, and I wasn't sure what we'd do next.

The freezer was close to empty, and we sure didn't have anything fresh in the fridge. It was like a science experiment in there, and I had to throw out anything that looked like an alien life form. When I came home from school on Monday, though, there was milk, cheese and salad stuff in the fridge, and Mackenzie was cooking spaghetti and meatballs. The kitchen was all steamed up, and that made me smile.

"I'm starving," I said. I hadn't taken any food to school, and I couldn't afford the cafeteria. "How'd you do this?"

Mackenzie smiled that sweet smile she had when she didn't feel scared or lost in the world. "I have survival skills."

I grabbed a carrot from the counter and chomped down on it. "Really? Like what?"

"I went downtown and bummed money from people."

"Panhandling?"

"You could call it that. I'm good at it sometimes."

"How much did you get?"

"Twenty-four dollars."

I smiled and gave her a hug. I'd been careful about being physical with her. I knew she liked me, but I remembered her rules. The first time I'd hugged her, she had stiffened and pulled away. This time she hugged me back. It felt good. I wanted to kiss her. But I didn't. I just didn't want to upset whatever it was we had.

"How does it feel? Begging from strangers?"

"I don't think about it. That's part of what survival skills are all about. Sometimes you just do what you have to do."

But I didn't like the thought of Mac out there on the street bumming change. "Maybe I can get a job."

"No, idiot. You gotta stay in school."

"Well, maybe a part-time job." I realized I would do just about anything to keep what we had going. But I was living in a bubble.

The spaghetti was heaven, and I filled my gut and then fed Ozzie from the new bag of dog food Mac had bought. That's when the doorbell rang.

At first I didn't answer it, but it kept ringing, and I knew whoever it was wasn't going to go away. And Ozzie had begun to bark, and I knew he wouldn't stop.

When I opened the door, I recognized him. The landlord. Mr. Powell. I'd met the guy about a dozen times before, but I didn't think he even knew my name. He scowled at me.

"Your father here?" he asked.

I shook my head.

"Your mother?"

"She's out too," I said.

Ozzie came over and stood beside me. He did one of the low growls he did sometimes when he felt threatened.

Mr. Powell looked over my shoulder and saw Mackenzie in the kitchen. Then he looked down at the hardwood floor in the entrance. "That damn dog's scratched up the floors."

"Sorry about that," I said.

Mr. Powell was trying to size up the situation, and he didn't like what he saw. "You guys don't ever bother to answer your phone?"

"We've been out a lot," I countered.

"Listen, kid. What's your name?"

"Cameron."

"Cameron, the rent is, like, three months overdue. I haven't heard from your mother or your father. This isn't good. Tell your parents they need to pay up or you have to move out of here. I'm sorry." He didn't look like he was sorry. "I'm running a business, you know. I ain't got no time for deadbeats."

And he left. Suddenly the meatballs in my stomach felt like hot lead.

I looked at Mac, and her glow was gone. The bubble had burst. I hugged her again, and this time it felt different. She hugged back, but it wasn't a warm happy hug.

So I guess dear old Dad hadn't been keeping up with the rent. I guess he'd been thinking about his exodus for a while. Of course, he wasn't thinking I'd be left here by myself. Or maybe he just wasn't thinking at all.

On Tuesday, I saw a police car pull up out front. I was sitting by the window doing my English homework, trying to write an essay about a poem by Shakespeare that begins, *When, in disgrace with fortune and men's eyes*. As the cop walked up to the house, I realized that Mr. Powell had probably decided he wasn't going to wait any longer for his money. Maybe he'd talked to the neighbors. Maybe he knew my parents weren't here anymore. I locked Ozzie in my bedroom so he wouldn't cause any trouble. Mackenzie heard me and asked, "What's up?"

"Just stay in your room for now. It's okay."

The doorbell rang, and I opened the door, trying to act cool. I had my English anthology in my hand.

"Hi," I said.

"Hi," he said. The cop was just a young guy, maybe mid-twenties. The uniform didn't quite fit right, and he seemed a little uncomfortable but was trying to act…well, like a cop.

"What's up?" I asked as nonchalantly as I could.

"Your parents here?"

"Not now, no."

"I'd like to speak with them. You expect them back soon?"

"They're out of town for a day or so."

He was scratching his jaw now, looking down at the ground. "Well, we had a call from the guy who owns this house. You rent, right?"

"Yeah. My parents do."

"Well, this Powell guy thinks there might be something not right going on here."

"Everything's cool here," I said. I held up my anthology, as if the fact that I had been reading Shakespeare somehow made everything on the level.

"Your landlord says the rent hasn't been paid. He thinks you might be living here on your own." He scratched his jaw again, and I could tell he didn't like confronting me like this. "And he thinks there might be drugs."

"No drugs," I said. "I swear." There was an awkward silence, and I heard Ozzie scratching at my bedroom door. I also thought I could hear something else. Another door opening and closing.

The young cop put his hands together in front of him. "Right. Maybe the guy's just paranoid. But if you haven't paid the rent, he can evict you."

"My dad said he was getting that all sorted out. He's had a bit of bad luck, but now things are coming together."

He nodded. "Sure. Let's leave it at that. I'll check in with the landlord, and I'll check back here in a couple of days to talk with your folks."

"Of course," I said. "Thanks."

"Take care."

I stood there for a minute as he walked back to his car. My brain couldn't get a grip on what we needed to do next. I let Ozzie out of the bedroom and gave him a hug. Then I went to talk to Mackenzie, but when I knocked on her door, she didn't answer. After the third knock, I broke one of her rules and opened it.

She was gone, and so was her famous suitcase. I ran to the back door. It was partly open, and Mackenzie was nowhere in sight.

## Chapter Eight

I put Ozzie on his leash, and we spent three hours looking for her. She wasn't in the park. She wasn't at the coffee shop. I asked other kids on the street, but no one had seen a girl with rolling luggage. I was cold and tired by the time ten o'clock rolled around.

I went home—or the place that had once been my home. I lay down on my bed and drifted into a restless sleep. I kept hoping I'd hear the front door open and she'd be back. But it didn't happen.

I cut school the next day and went searching again.

The day ended with another failed attempt and another fitful night's sleep. I felt alone and deserted. And scared.

I knew that if Mackenzie didn't want to be found, I wouldn't be able to find her. So I went back to school, heartbroken, tired and already feeling like the old Cameron—pissed off at everything.

I came home that day to find a padlock bolted onto the door, a lot of stuff from the house out on the lawn and Ozzie tied to the railing. I sat down on the front steps beside him, put my head between my legs and took a deep breath. I felt like I was going to puke. I guess I could have tried calling my mom— or Nick, even. Or my dad's cell phone.

But they were the ones who'd gotten me into this mess. At this moment, I hated them all.

Anger replaced the fear, I guess. Ozzie was nervous. He was actually shaking, and I'd only seen him like that a couple of times before, when he was threatened by some big nasty dogs. I gave him a good hug and told him it was all going to be okay. Then I emptied my backpack of schoolbooks and rooted through the piles on the lawn until I found some of my clothes and a flashlight, and I stuffed them into the pack.

If I'd had a cell phone, I would have taken a picture of me and the junk scattered on the front lawn. A portrait of what it looks like when your life falls apart. When everything goes down the toilet. But my phone had stopped working awhile back, and I didn't have the money to get a new one. All I had was a five-dollar bill in my pocket.

That was it. My backpack with some stuff, my dog and me.

Maybe I should have broken a window at the back and crawled back into the house. But I couldn't bring myself to do it. I only had one thought.

I had to find Mackenzie. Maybe she'd given up on me, but I hadn't given up on her. And now I needed her more than ever.

Ozzie looked worried. Worried about me. "It's okay, boy. Now it's just you and me."

My legs felt funny as we began to walk down the street. It would be dark soon, and I'd have to figure something out. But I couldn't stay here. This was no longer my home. And, as far as I was concerned, I no longer had parents.

Ozzie seemed to know where we were going—to the park, then to the street that led downtown. I hit the coffee shop where I'd found Mackenzie sleeping and then went and talked to some of the kids I'd seen panhandling.

Most were pretty wary of my asking questions about Mac. I couldn't tell the ones who might actually know her and lied about it from the ones who really didn't know her. Then, as it got later, I realized I needed to start figuring out where I was going to spend the night. I doubled back to the coffee shop, but it was empty. I asked some of the kids on the street where I could crash for the night, but they didn't know. I guess they didn't trust me. I didn't look or act like them. And they were used to all kinds of weirdos asking questions. Some of them didn't trust the dog.

So Ozzie and I kept walking, away from the bright lights and stores, until we came to an empty storefront that had once been a bakery. It was dark and empty. The front door was locked, but a side door into the basement was open.

Someone had busted the lock. It was pitch-black as Ozzie and I walked inside. I dug out my flashlight and looked around.

The place had been royally trashed. There were crumpled beer cans and broken liquor bottles. I wondered if the partiers would come back, and that made me want to get the hell out of there. But where would I go?

I had Ozzie. I'd have to take my chances. I saw an old mattress in the corner and a blanket. I lay down and folded my body into the fetal position. I was scared, yeah. And I lay there wondering if Mackenzie was holed up in some place like this. Alone and cold and scared.

## Chapter Nine

It was a long, cold night. When I woke up in the morning, I could see my breath. I looked around the basement. It was not a place I wanted to spend another night in. I was starving. I had no plan. I thought about going to school and bumming some money for cafeteria food, but I had a feeling it would go badly. Besides, I looked terrible. And what would I do with Ozzie?

All I could do was head out onto the street. I walked downtown, and though I'd been here many times before, it looked different to me now. Busy people all going somewhere. Jobs, school, stores. I wasn't one of them. I was going nowhere, and I felt like the biggest loser on the planet.

I walked a few blocks more, back to the coffee shop. Outside the place, I bumped into Ethan Sparks, a kid I knew from school.

"What are you doing here?" he asked.

"It's a long story. Have you seen Mackenzie?"

"Not recently. She's been gone for a while, and some of us are worried."

"Us?"

"You know." It sank in. The rumors about Ethan, that he was pretty much on his own.

"She was at my house for a while," I said. "But I got kicked out."

Ethan looked shocked. "Wait a minute. Do you mean what I think you mean?"

"I'm not sure what you think I mean, but yeah, I've been booted out. I've got nowhere to live. Me and Ozzie."

Ethan looked more than a little concerned. "You going to school today?"

"Looking like this?"

"Yeah. You do look like something your dog hauled out of the garbage. No offense."

I was beginning to see Ethan for what he really was. A lifeline.

"Ethan," I said, "I'm in a messed-up place. Got any advice? Got anything?"

He looked intently at me. I read genuine concern. "Yeah. Go home. Say you're sorry for whatever you did. Kiss ass. Do whatever. You don't want to be here."

"It's not that easy. Besides, I gotta find Mac. She ran off from my house when the cops showed up."

"And I'd like to see you find her. She's a good girl."

"Then tell me what to do."

Ethan didn't say anything at first. Then he looked me in the eye. "A few of us have been crashing at an apartment owned by a guy we call Crazy Eddy. Eddy *is* crazy, but he's fairly harmless. I've been sleeping on my cousin's couch this week, but that's not gonna last long. He's got a new girlfriend moving in. So if there's room, Eddy'll take me in. Hell, he'll take in just about anyone. You can only crash there from midnight to six in the morning, but it's better than the street. You've got to be clean. No drugs. Eddy used to have a habit, and he kicked it after he got busted. But he wants twenty bucks a night from whoever he takes in."

"I don't have that."

"Well, then, you do what you have to do."

"Like what?"

"Well, you see kids panhandling for money. Learn to work it."

"I've never done that."

"It's no fun, believe me. Look, here's ten bucks. All you have to do is scrounge the rest. I gotta go, but I'm around. You got a cell?"

"No."

"Man, you are desperate. Eddy's just above the coffee shop. Apartment five. Tell him I sent you. Me and Eddy are tight. But you'll have to have the twenty bucks, and don't ask him for food or anything. He hates that."

"What about the dog?"

"Hard to say with Eddy. Could go either way."

Ethan walked off, but then turned to look back at me. The look said he was worried. He was a good guy, and it was comforting to know I had at least one person on the street worried about my sorry ass.

## Chapter Ten

I couldn't do it at first. Beg for money.
I really couldn't. I hung out behind a
donut shop and waited to see what came
out the back door, hoping there was
food headed for a Dumpster or something. My instincts were good. Around
noon, the unsold baking from the day
before was tossed. I can't tell you how
good they tasted. Chocolate donuts.

Blueberry muffins. Enough for me and Ozzie, and I stashed some in my pack. Not exactly health food, but it was a start.

In the afternoon, I knew I had to get up my courage to talk to strangers. My line was lame, and I felt like a really bad actor. "Get a job," one guy in a suit said. "Get off the street and stop bothering people," one finely dressed woman said. When I saw cops coming my way, I held my head up and walked on by. The best I could do was mumble something to people passing by, and once in a while someone would hand me a quarter or a couple of dimes without making eye contact. It was brutal. Sometimes it was just nickles. Who the hell gives a homeless person nickles? But it was sinking in. I was homeless. And pretty helpless when it came to bumming money from people.

By six o'clock I had $23, but it had taken me almost all day to get it. And ten of it had come from Ethan. I headed to the coffee shop, tied up Ozzie outside and went in for a coffee and sandwich. Yeah. Kids hung out here because you could get coffee and an egg-salad sandwich for $2.99, and they didn't charge tax. I was afraid to leave Ozzie alone, so I took my meager meal outside and sat down on the sidewalk, my back against the wall. I tried begging some more but had no luck. I just didn't have it in me.

At 11:45 I went in the door beside the coffee shop and up the stairs. I knocked on the door of apartment five. Crazy Eddy was wearing a bathrobe and had a shower cap on his head. He was maybe thirty-five and had a bulging stomach and kind of bugged-out eyes.

"Ethan said I might be able to crash here tonight," I said.

"You got twenty bucks?"

I showed him a baggie with the ten and a bunch of change.

"Okay," he said. Then he looked down at Ozzie, who was sitting quietly beside me. "Who's this?" Eddy asked.

"His name's Ozzie."

"I don't usually take dogs."

"Ozzie's the sweetest dog you'll ever meet. I promise."

Eddy bent down, grabbed Ozzie's muzzle and put his face right up to the dog's in a pretty aggressive way. But Ozzie didn't flinch. Eddy stayed like that for a couple of seconds, and I almost thought he was going to hurt Ozzie. But then he patted Oz on the head and stood up. "Sleep on the floor— you and the dog. Not on the furniture. And no eating my food."

I followed Eddy into the apartment, and he pointed me toward the living room while he traipsed off to another room and slammed the door. When I walked into the living room, I saw three other kids there. Two were already in sleeping bags and conked out. A third, a girl, was sitting with her back to me, reading in the dim light.

"Hey," I said.

She turned. It was Mackenzie. "Cameron."

I didn't know what to say. Ozzie recognized her and licked her face. "I thought I'd lost you," I said.

I sat down beside her. "You did," she whispered. "I was scared. Sorry I split like that. I had to. I can't believe you're here."

"Ethan told me about Eddy."

"I hate this place. But it's all I've got for now. We can't sit here and talk though. He'll hear us, and these guys are trying to sleep. We'll talk tomorrow."

I nodded, settled my pack by the wall and curled up beside her, with Ozzie at our feet.

The next day I couldn't bring myself to go to school. I was afraid of losing Mackenzie again. At six AM, Eddy started banging pots together and shouting, "Time to get up and out on the street, people." And of course he meant it.

Mac left her suitcase behind. "Eddy said it's okay," she said. "But I think he goes through it when I'm gone."

"Is this place safe?" I asked. "I mean, for you?"

"Eddy's never touched me."

Which was good news. But after she'd said it, I realized her answer implied that other men had. Mac read the worry in my face. "Come on. We gotta go."

Mackenzie showed me where to score some better grub. We went inside a busy McDonald's and scavenged food from trays on the tables after people had left. We downed hash browns and half-eaten Egg McMuffins until we were found out and politely asked to leave.

"If we want to stay at Eddy's again, we've gotta scrounge forty bucks between us," Mackenzie said.

"Right now that sounds like a fortune."

"Watch me," she said.

I watched, expecting that a girl asking for money would work like a charm. But it didn't.

I tried my hand at it for a while and only got pocket change. By late afternoon we'd only scrounged $26. It was a long, weird, frustrating day. "How long has this been your life?" I asked.

"A couple of years," she said. "It never gets any easier."

"You take the money," I insisted. "All of it. Go get a sandwich and go to Eddy's."

"And leave you?"

"I got a crash pad down the road. The old Midtown Bakery."

She scowled. "The basement, right? That hellhole?"

"You make it sound so bleak," I said jokingly, trying to lighten things up.

"I've checked in there before. I'll join you. We'll have better luck tomorrow."

I couldn't talk her out of it. She didn't want to leave me on my own. I realized this was an amazingly tough girl.

On the way there, some punks stopped us and asked us for smokes. When we said we didn't have any, one of them started thumping me on the chest with a finger and said he didn't like trash like me on the street. Ozzie barked at them and showed his teeth, and they backed off.

When we were almost there, a car stopped beside us. A man rolled down the window. "That you, Mackenzie?"

"Keep walking," she said. She didn't turn to look at him.

"Mackenzie, sweetheart," he said. "You must be cold. The car's nice and warm. Why don't you join me for a ride?"

She stopped and looked at him. In a fake-polite voice, she answered, "Not tonight. I can't. I'm busy."

I got a good look at the face of the guy now. He wore glasses and had a tie on. He looked at me and sneered. Then he just drove off.

"What was that all about?" I asked.

"I don't want to talk about it," she said.

We made our way into the basement of the old bakery and settled in as best we could. My fear was that troublemakers—maybe those punks from the street—would find us in the middle of the night. I could barely sleep.

And Ozzie felt the danger too. Every time I looked up, he was standing guard at the door to the basement. When I lay back down with my back to Mac, she put her arm around me and held me tight. It almost made the whole crappy day worthwhile.

# Chapter Eleven

In the morning we woke up to sunlight coming through the basement window. I felt disoriented and confused. It was cold, and I was hungry. Mackenzie sat up and let out a sigh. She looked discouraged.

"We're gonna figure something out so we never have to do this again,"

I said. I meant it, although I didn't really have a plan at all.

We stumbled out of the basement and went to the coffee shop for breakfast. We splurged on some real food. Mac insisted. Ozzie got the scraps, but I knew I had to get him some real dog food. I really hadn't thought any of this through. But I was determined now to keep Mac with me. We'd survive somehow. All three of us.

After breakfast we took to the street. "Listen, we need to split up," Mac said. "People are more likely to give money to a girl alone than two of us."

"Right," I said. "But I'm not letting you out of my sight."

So we did opposite corners of a busy downtown street, away from where the other street kids were. I tried a number of different lines. "Excuse me, could you spare some money so I can get a meal?" "Please, sir, I'm trying to get back home.

I need money for bus fare." And "Miss, could you help me out? I'm cold and need a place to stay tonight."

Most folks just ignored me or carved an arc around me as they walked by. Few people would make eye contact with me, but many would look at Ozzie, loyal and calm by my side. Some patted the dog and didn't give me anything. Some folks patted the dog and gave me a quarter. The results were meager. But then it sunk in.

A mother with two little kids approached and began to steer her little ones away from me. "Please," I said, holding out an empty coffee cup. "My dog hasn't eaten for two days. Can you spare some change so I can buy him dog food?"

She stopped in her tracks and opened her purse. She looked at the dog and then at me. She smiled and handed me a ten-dollar bill. She even let her kids pat Ozzie's head. "Thank you," I said. "Thank you so much."

When they had gone, I looked across the street at Mackenzie. She had been watching. She waved and gave me a big smile, and I suddenly felt like the world was a much kinder place than I had thought. And I'd learned my lesson. People were more likely to give me money to feed my dog than to feed me. If we were lucky, Ozzie would help us pay the rent and keep us all fed.

By mid-afternoon, Mac and I had enough money to stay the night at Eddy's. We went to the public library to warm up for a bit, but I hated leaving Ozzie out in the cold, lashed to a post, for long. We bought some food at the grocery store and snacked on carrots and celery with peanut butter. As the long but good day came to a close, we found our way to Eddy's and cooked macaroni and cheese at one AM, then fell asleep on the living room floor, next to Ethan and a couple of other kids who were already snoring.

In the morning, Eddy was sitting in the kitchen, feeding Ozzie and patting his back. They looked like old chums. As Mac and I got ready to hit the streets, she said, "Cameron, you have to get your ass back in school today. You can't lose that. I made a big mistake in dropping out. You can't do the same."

"But I don't care about school anymore."

"Well, you should. I wish I hadn't had to quit."

"I'm afraid of losing you."

"I'm not going anywhere. I'll do the usual routine and work the street. We'll regroup this afternoon. It will be fine."

"What about Oz?" I asked.

Eddy was listening to the conversation. He jumped in and said, "The dog can stay here. I like him."

Mac was looking at Ozzie, who had just had his first real meal in a couple of days. "Yeah," she said. "He should stay here, and we'll get him this afternoon. You'll need your star performer if you want to work the crowd."

Eddy smiled. He looked mellower than before.

If Mac hadn't seemed so certain, I wouldn't have gone along with it. But I didn't have a better plan. I decided I could trust Mac to be there at the end of the school day. I could see that Ozzie would be all right here. And I realized that if I was gonna make it in this weird new world, I'd have to trust someone. Even if it had to be Crazy Eddy.

Then something else hit me like lightning. If Mac wanted me back in school, maybe deep down she wanted to get herself back in school too. "Tell you what," I said. "I'll go to school if you come with me. You can talk to the guidance counselor, Mr. Brewster, about dropping back in. We'll both work the streets when school is over, but we'll have someplace to hang out during the day. Someplace warm and safe."

I expected to get massive resistance, but she surprised me. "I've been thinking about that for quite a while, but I never had the courage to just walk in through the doors by myself."

"But now you're not by yourself."

# Chapter Twelve

I thought she was going to chicken out about school. She chattered nervously all the way there. We dropped by the school office, and I introduced her to Mr. Brewster. Brewster had given me plenty of crap in the last couple of years, but he'd always seemed like a straight shooter. Like I said, I had to trust someone. So I decided to trust him.

When I went off to class, Mackenzie was smiling and answering Brewster's questions. Things were going well.

I was having a hard time concentrating and even staying awake in my classes. Missing just a few days had put me behind. I also noticed the other kids looking at me funny. Yeah, I'd been sleeping in my clothes. On Eddy's floor and in that damn bakery basement.

I met up with Mac at lunchtime. She looked a little nervous but said she was okay. We had enough money left to split a meal between us, and cafeteria food had never tasted so good. Davis Conlon saw us sitting together and shook his head and smiled an obnoxious, condescending smile. I'd try to keep us clear of him and his friends, but I knew that pretty soon some things about Mac and me would be school news.

As we approached Eddy's place in the afternoon, I could hear Ozzie barking.

The door was unlocked, and we walked right in. Eddy, still in his bathrobe, was wide-eyed, yelling and smashing dishes on the kitchen floor. He looked up when we came in. Then he looked down at the smashed plates on the floor and seemed surprised, as if he didn't know who had done it. Ozzie was frantic. He ran to me, and I bent over and gave him a hug. Eddy now looked embarrassed and confused. "Sorry," he said and turned to go to his bedroom.

Mac had hung back by the door, and she looked scared. I was beginning to wonder how safe our crash pad was and if Crazy Eddy was as harmless as we had thought.

Back on the street, our luck was good. We worked the corners again. The after-work crowd was ready to ante up to feed a dog, although some people who had given money to me the day before looked at me differently now and just walked on by. I was always cheered up if someone who gave me money stopped to speak to me, like one older woman did. "I'm Ruth," she said. "Ruth Goldbloom. What's your name?"

"Cam," I said. "And this is Ozzie."

She smiled. "Everything going okay?" It seemed like a really odd question to be asking a homeless person. I almost gave her a really snarky answer. But I didn't.

"As good as can be expected," I said.

"Good," was all she said. She patted Ozzie again and walked away.

I kept an eye on Mac across the street, and in less than two hours we had enough money for some food and another night, maybe our last one, at Eddy's. Other kids would be there, so I was pretty sure we'd be okay, and, besides, we had nowhere else to go.

Unfortunately, our good luck panhandling had attracted the attention of a policeman. "I can fine you both for panhandling, you know. It's against the law."

We both said nothing.

"You have a license for the dog?" he asked.

I shook my head.

He looked us over, then Ozzie. "A couple of store owners made a complaint. I'm obliged to follow up."

"What are they complaining about?" I asked, trying not to sound hostile.

"People don't like having you begging them for money."

"What are we supposed to do?" Mackenzie asked.

The cop looked annoyed, but he took a deep breath. "Look, you've got a warning, okay?" And he walked away.

But we were good for the day. We had enough money. We went to the coffee shop, and Ozzie dutifully sat down on the sidewalk while we tied him to a bicycle rack.

"You'll get used to it," Mac said.

"Used to what?"

"The cops. They don't really want to arrest us."

"But they can if they want to, right?"

"Yeah. But if we're careful, and if we keep an eye out for them, I think we'll be okay."

After the cop had spoken to us, I'd realized just how vulnerable we were. No one was looking out for us. Although we hadn't finished our coffee, I had a funny feeling. "Come on. Let's go," I said.

When we got out on the sidewalk, Ozzie was gone. He was nowhere to be seen. I felt a wave of panic, and my mind went numb. Ozzie wouldn't have run off, even if he hadn't been tied up. We had to find him. Had someone stolen him, or had the police taken him?

Maybe Mackenzie was wrong about the cops.

"We have to find him," I said, desperation in my voice.

At the police station uptown, we were greeted by a bored-looking woman in uniform. She listened to our story, then said, "Sorry, dogs aren't our business. You have to talk to animal control." She checked her watch. "They're closed now, but open at eight in the morning. If your dog got picked up, he'd be there."

I wanted to go there right away, but Mackenzie said they wouldn't open the doors for us. "He'll be okay for one night if he's there. We'll go first thing in the morning."

"I love my dog," I said.

"I know you do," she said. "We'll find him."

We decided to go back to Eddy's and head out first thing in the morning.

Eddy was calmer than he'd been earlier. "Where's Ozzie?" he asked.

When I told him what had happened, he went on another rant, this time about the cops. Then things quieted down and I slept fitfully, worried that maybe I'd lost Ozzie forever.

## Chapter Thirteen

Mackenzie and I used what little money we had left to take a bus to the industrial park on the other side of the river. That's where the animal-control center was. We were standing outside the door when it opened a few minutes after eight. A woman at the reception desk heard our story and motioned to a sour-looking guy in a uniform. "Deacon, take these hobos on the tour."

Deacon had a big set of keys, and he led us out of the small office and into a concrete nightmare of howling and snarling dogs and unimaginable smells. There were dozens of dogs in here. We walked down one row, then another. Then another. It was like a horrible prison for lost pets. Deacon didn't seem to have much time for us, and he seemed downright angry that we didn't just pick any old mutt and say, "Yeah, that's him," so he could get rid of us. We neared the end of the last row. I was having a hard time breathing. Mackenzie held on to my arm and tightened her grip when she knew I was afraid we wouldn't find him.

I'd had enough of the smell of dog crap and pee and really needed to get out of there for fresh air, but I was afraid they might not let me back in. I thought I was gonna puke.

But then, there he was. Ozzie. He was lying on the cold concrete floor, his tail tucked in and his head down. He didn't see us at first. "Ozzie," I said. He sprang to life, got to his feet and began wagging his tail. I shoved my hands through the bars and held his gorgeous face.

"That's him," Mac told Deacon. "Can you open the door so we can get him out of here?"

Deacon acted as if she'd just asked him if we could throw his mother over a cliff. He leaned over and looked at the tag on the bars of the cage. "Says here he was found abandoned on Spring Street."

"He wasn't abandoned," I said. "We were inside a coffee shop for, like, ten minutes."

"Whatever," he said. "Yeah sure, you can take him. Just go pay the fine first. Two hundred bucks."

I stood up and looked at Mac, then at the man in uniform. "We don't have that kind of money, sir," I said as politely as I could.

He cleared his throat and looked at us, sizing us up. He knew what he was looking at—a couple of sorry-ass street kids. But that didn't exactly inspire compassion in this old buzzard who spent his days inhaling the pungent smell of dog crap. "You'll have to find it. That's the fine. Everyone has to pay if they want their pooch back."

"What if we can't get the money?" Mackenzie asked.

"We hold the dog for ten days. Like I say, the official story is he was abandoned. No tags or nothing. We get hundreds of dogs like him down here. He ain't no different from the rest."

I looked around at "the rest." A howling, barking, dirty zoo of impris-oned animals, some who would be rescued and some, I knew, who would not. "And after ten days?"

"We put him up for adoption," Deacon said flatly. Then he looked up at the ceiling and added, "But only a small number of these mangy hounds ever find a home. Especially older dogs like this."

It was unbearable to think of Ozzie living with someone else. I felt the blood drain from my head as I asked the next necessary question. "What happens if he doesn't get adopted?"

Deacon just put his hands in the air. He didn't have to say it. I knew what would happen. The same thing that was likely to happen to most of the sad and hopeless dogs in this hellhole. "Can't we just take him outside for a walk?" Mac asked. "We'll bring him back, I promise. Then we'll go get the money. Please."

Deacon looked at her, and for a split second I thought the hard-bitten old geezer was going to drop his guard and be human. But even if he'd felt something, he wasn't buying. "Sorry, sweetheart. Can't do it."

I was ready to tackle this guy. I really was. I figured I could knock him down, Mac could release Oz, and we would run. But the saner part of my brain was telling me we'd be in deeper trouble if we did that and might never see Ozzie again. It was one of the hardest things I'd ever done to walk away from my dog as he watched us leave.

Outside, it had begun to snow. We walked a long way before we came to a pay phone at a gas station. It's not until you find yourself without a cell phone and living on the street that you realize how few pay phones are left. I called my mom's cell, and she answered. I explained about Ozzie. I begged her for the money.

At first she didn't say anything. Then she said, "I'm sorry, Cameron, I can't.

If Nick found out, he'd be really mad. We're just working things out. I can't take the chance. I can't do something behind his back."

"Jesus, Mom. This is Ozzie we're talking about. It's only two hundred dollars."

"I'm sorry, Cam. I can't. Some nice family will adopt him. Cam, I'm worried about you. Come back home."

But she didn't mean home, I knew. She meant Nick's place. It wasn't going to happen.

I used the rest of our change to call my dad out west, but all I got was a message saying his number was no longer active. With almost no money left, we had to hitchhike back downtown. That taught me another lesson about life on the street. Drivers don't like picking up hitchhikers when it's snowing.

# Chapter Fourteen

Back on Spring Street, we started to panhandle, but there weren't many people out in the snow and wind. I tried telling the truth about our situation to the people walking by, but no one wanted to stop and listen. Another rule of the street. The more desperate you really are, the less likely people are to stop and listen.

We gave up early and knocked on Eddy's door. As usual, he was in his bathrobe. The TV was blasting in the background—some reality show about rich housewives. "Too early," Eddy said. "Come back later."

"Eddy," Mac said, "they took our dog. He's in the dog pound. We need your help."

"Ozzie? They took Ozzie?"

I nodded. "We need two hundred dollars to bust him out of there. Can you help us?"

I could see that he was genuinely concerned. I think he really liked the dog. "Two hundred bucks? Are you crazy? Where would I get that kind of money?" Then he shook his head. "Poor Ozzie."

No. Eddy couldn't help us. But he did let us in early, and though he told us we had to stay in the kitchen until his TV show was over, he said we could crash there for free that night. Eddy was crazy, and he was unpredictable, but he had a heart.

In the morning, we still didn't know what to do. Mac convinced me we should go to school. Maybe if we talked to enough kids, someone would be able to help. The snowplows were out, but the sidewalks hadn't been shoveled. We had wet feet and cold hands by the time we approached the front door of the school. Mackenzie stopped suddenly. "I just had an idea," she said. "I think I know a couple of people who can help. Real dog lovers."

"Great," I said. "Let's go."

She shook her head. "No, if I'm going to convince them, I have to go alone. If you were there, it wouldn't work. Besides, it's a ways off. Bus fare. I only have enough for one of us. That's me."

"I thought we decided we were going to stick together. Look out for each other."

"I know. But this is for Ozzie. You go to school. Talk to some kids. See if anyone can help. But I'll go see my friend, and I think it will work."

"I don't like you leaving."

"I know. But it's going to be okay." Then she leaned forward and kissed me on the mouth. "It's going to be okay. I promise. Go to school. Be good. I'll be here when you come out." She started to walk away.

"But tell me where you're going," I said.

She didn't stop. "I'll be back," she said. "Then we'll get Ozzie."

If she hadn't seemed so certain, so positive, so upbeat, I wouldn't have let her walk away. And then she was gone, and the bell was ringing. I tried to keep my mind locked on the light at the end of the tunnel. Freeing Ozzie, moving on to…I didn't know what.

I tried talking to a few kids about "borrowing" some cash. I explained about my dog. I thought people would care. But I'd become one of those students who came to school every day looking ratty from sleeping on somebody's couch or crashing wherever they could. Kids like Ethan and Emma March and Mackenzie. Like them, I was now trying to bum money from classmates. We'd all been observed and labeled and made fun of and, ultimately, ignored.

Even though my requests for money didn't go well, I stayed focused on the positive energy I'd seen in Mac that morning. And the fact that she had kissed me. And that she was coming back. We would free Ozzie. I knew it. And so, strange as it may sound, I had a pretty good day at school. I wrote an in-class essay about a poem by Walt Whitman.

I passed a history test, and I stayed awake through the day.

The bell was about to ring, and the day would be over. I'd be back with Mac. As I shoved my books into my locker, I noticed Davis Conlon sneering at me from across the hall. I ignored the creep. I was getting good at that. The girl beside my locker, Jenna, was talking to a couple of her friends. As I closed my locker, I said, "Hi, Jenna, how's it going?"

She gave me a funny look, but she answered, "It's going okay, I guess. How about you?"

So I decided to tell her about my dog problem. She and her friends listened. But I could see from their eyes that they didn't believe me. When I got to the part about asking to borrow some money, one of the girls rolled her eyes. Jenna just said, "I'll see what I can do. Maybe tomorrow." But I knew she didn't mean it. Then came the kicker. "Cameron," she said, "I hate to say this, but man, you smell really bad. When was the last time you had a shower?" The other two girls giggled.

I'm not even sure she meant to be mean. But she was right. I stunk. And it hit me then just how far apart our worlds were, even though our lockers were side by side and we were in the same school. "I know," I said, and I walked away.

As I made my way through the noisy afternoon hallways, I realized that I was different now from most of the other kids. That I'd maybe never be one of them again. No home, no bedroom, no parents to come home to. Yeah, I felt like crying. And I started to worry that something might have happened to Mackenzie. That she wouldn't be outside waiting for me. *Please God, please let Mac be there*, I prayed silently. It was something I hadn't done in a long time.

The sun was shining brightly on the snow outside. My eyes were having a hard time adjusting to the light. I took a deep breath of the fresh air and looked around.

And then she was there. Sneaking up behind me and putting her arms around me. "Surprise," she said. I spun around. I smiled. I tried to kiss her, but she pulled away.

"Sorry," I said.

"Don't be. Look." She had a wad of twenties in her hand.

"Wow. Your friend?"

"Yeah. Let's go. Let's get the bus. Let's go free Ozzie."

I guess I didn't want to ask too many questions. Maybe there really had been a friend. Maybe it was something personal—an old boyfriend. I don't know. I just knew we had the money and I should be happy.

Ozzie saw us walking down the corridor. Deacon almost seemed glad to see us. "See?" he said. "Happy ending."

In an empty lot in the industrial park, we let Ozzie run free and played in the snow. We threw snowballs, and he chased them. We pretended to chase him, and he ran in circles. And then we hitchhiked back to town, getting a ride all the way there with an old hippie in a van who told stories of "the good old days" all the way.

And we had money left over to crash at Eddy's. Eddy seemed super happy to see Ozzie back. In the morning, he promised to stay "cool" and take good care of Ozzie while we went to school.

And yes, Mackenzie and I went to school.

Mr. Brewster called us both to his office from our first class. I thought we were in some kind of trouble. But it wasn't that.

"Some of the students," he said, "have expressed concern about the two of you."

I assumed their concern was that we both smelled bad, but I didn't ask.

"I had a meeting with the principal, and we thought we could help out a little." He handed us some slips of paper. "Hang on to these. Take them to the cafeteria. You'll get a breakfast and a lunch. No big deal. But it should help."

"Thanks," we both said in unison.

"And you'll be allowed to use the gym showers."

Maybe the stink had done some good. Maybe Jenna and her friends, or whoever, really did have some concern. Food and showers. Things were looking up. Maybe it was all coming together.

# Chapter Fifteen

I badgered Mackenzie about who had given her the money to spring Ozzie. I wanted to know who it was and how we could pay this person back in some way. But every time I brought it up, she was quiet and mysterious. "Don't worry about it. It's okay," she said. But there was something weird about it.

School was, well, school. But we were hanging in there. We had breakfast and lunch there, and the showers were great. Mac and I both found time to get our homework done during the day, and sometimes we stayed after school at the library to study. I was back to thinking about my New Year's resolution. All I had to do was finish this year and get through one more, and I'd graduate. There was light at the end of the tunnel.

We'd given up panhandling on Spring Street. The cops there knew us too well. We'd been warned about getting arrested, and I was afraid animal control might show up and grab Ozzie again.

Mac had convinced me we shouldn't work so close together. She said it drew too much attention. Instead, we worked a few blocks apart from each other and only after school and into the evening. It was getting warmer, but the rainy days were killers. And the worse the weather, the less likely people were to give us any change. I made a little cardboard sign that said *Please Help Me Feed My Dog.* Some people became "regulars" and would actually stop to say hi and pet Ozzie. But no matter how politely I chatted with people and how lovable Ozzie was, I always ended up with less money than Mackenzie. "It's because I'm a girl," she said. "People feel sorry for me."

A lot of nights, I'd have only eight or ten dollars, and Mac would have enough to cover for me. She always seemed to have enough for us to crash another night at Eddy's. Yeah, Eddy always wanted the money, although by now it seemed like we were part of his family. It was one hell of a weird family, but it was all we had. Ethan was there many nights, and he never wanted to talk about where he'd spent the nights he didn't show.

Mac was late sometimes for our evening rendezvous in front of the coffee shop, but she always got there eventually. I guessed she kept panhandling until she was sure we'd have enough to crash at Eddy's. Sometimes she looked tired. Sometimes discouraged. She never seemed to want to talk about her time on the street. I worried about her. I worried about us.

"Maybe we can find some other place," I said. "Some place just a little more sane."

"Eddy's is more than just a little weird," she admitted. "But I think it's all we have for now. Believe me, it could be worse."

I remembered sleeping in the basement of the bakery and knew she was right.

Two weeks later, just when I thought everything was going really well, a couple of girls at school started picking on Mac. Davis Conlon had started spreading a rumor that Mac was hanging out with Jenna's boyfriend. He'd implied, of course, that it was more than hanging out. Jenna was one of those girls who'd had maybe twelve boyfriends in the last year. Her trademark move was to steal someone else's boyfriend by having sex with him and then, as soon as she'd stolen him away, drop him like a hot potato and move on. She was a real piece of work. So now that it was rumored Mac had pulled the same move on her, she wanted revenge. Jenna didn't even seem to care whether it was true.

I was headed toward the cafeteria to meet up with Mac when I heard Jenna screaming. By the time I got there, a crowd of students had formed a circle around them. Jenna was screeching at Mac, who was just standing there looking frightened and pale. I tried to push my way through to get her out of there, but Davis, the bastard, grabbed me from behind and pulled me backward. I tried to slug him, but as I turned around, I lost my balance and fell to the floor. Nobody tried to help me up.

When I got to my feet and pushed through the mob, Jenna was down on the floor and Mac was on top of her, delivering a serious blow to her face. A couple of Jenna's friends grabbed Mac's hair and tried to pull her off. She screamed and flailed out at them. All the while, the idiot crowd cheered and yelled. Someone grabbed me again and pulled me backward and onto the floor. Somebody else kicked me in the ribs. I was ready to start punching anyone who got in my way.

By the time I was back on my feet, Mr. Brewster and the school security guard had arrived. Brewster grabbed hold of Mackenzie and pinned her arms, then began walking her to his office. He was glaring at the other students.

I followed them to the office and barged in. Mac was in a chair, looking angry and ready to explode. Mr. Brewster didn't ask me to leave. He just closed the door and sat down at his desk. I gave Mac a hug. She was tense and shaking with anger. "It's going to be all right," I whispered.

"No, it isn't," she said. "I'm never coming back here."

# Chapter Sixteen

Mr. Brewster listened to Mac's story about what had happened and said he was sorry but had to at least give her a suspension. She just sat there silently and didn't say a word in her defense. I tried to reason with Brewster, but he said his decision was final.

"The two of you head home for the day. It's best to have you out of the building."

"Sure," I said. I stood up and tried to take Mac's hand, but she pulled it back.

Outside the school, Mac was still shaking with rage. "Home," she said. "Did you hear that? He knows we don't have any home to go to."

"This will all blow over," I said.

"Cam, this is all your fault," she said, glaring at me.

"No, it's not."

"Yeah, it is. You convinced me going back to school was the right thing. It wasn't. You think stuff like that hasn't happened to me before? I'm never going back."

She stopped and looked at me. "I think I need to be alone for a while." She started to walk away.

"Wait," I said.

"I just want you to leave me alone," she said. And then she began to run.

I wanted to follow her, but I had seen something in her eyes. She was on fire with rage over what had just happened, and she was angry at the world. She was pissed off at me, even though it wasn't my fault. I had to give her some space.

It was a long, hard afternoon and a worse evening. I looked for her everywhere on the streets. No luck. She didn't meet me at the coffee shop that night and she wasn't at Eddy's at midnight. No one had seen her. I didn't have Eddy's twenty bucks. I'd only scrounged a mere nine dollars. But he let me stay. "Just this once," he said. "And don't tell anyone I'm letting you do this."

The next morning I felt terrible. I was worried about Mac, and to be honest, I felt abandoned. What if she'd taken off to another city? What if she was gone, and I never saw her again?

I had a big hollow feeling in my chest. It was like my heart was about to burst.

I didn't go to school. Maybe I'd never go to school again either. Maybe my optimism about the future was a load of crap. I left Eddy's with Ozzie, thinking that maybe I'd never go back there either, never spend another night sleeping on that hard living room floor.

Ozzie and I trekked all over the city. I knew it was hopeless. By late afternoon, I even thought about going to the police. I was worried something had happened to her. But I didn't trust the cops. Maybe they'd see that Ozzie had no license and try to take him away. And I wasn't sure there was much they could do. Or would do. I was on my own again.

By evening I had made a wide circuit around much of the downtown, and I was back on Spring Street. I didn't have a cent and was prepping myself for a night at Hell's Bakery. I was sitting on the sidewalk in front of the coffee shop when a car skidded to a stop. The door opened, and the driver shoved a girl out onto the street. It was Mac.

Ozzie sprang away from me, and I lost my grip on his leash. I was getting to my feet as Oz leaped through the open door of the car. He lunged at the man's arm and bit hard into the guy's hand. I'd never seen Ozzie bite anyone before. As Mac lay crumpled at the curb, the driver struggled to get free of Ozzie. He finally managed to push him back, and the car began to move forward. The door started to swing shut. Ozzie hung on at first, but then the door hit him. He yelped and fell back. The driver sat up straight, and the car sped away.

I knelt down beside Mackenzie as she tried to sit up. She was crying, and her face was bruised and bleeding. It wasn't just from being pushed out of the car. Pedestrians were stopping, and a woman stooped down to ask if we needed help. I hugged Mac to me, and Ozzie began to lick her face. "I gotta get you to the hospital," I said to her.

"No," she said.

"She needs to get to emergency," I heard the woman say. "I've got a car close by." As she leaned closer to Mackenzie, I recognized her as Ruth Goldbloom, the woman who had sometimes given me money and stopped to talk. "Can you walk?" she asked.

Mackenzie nodded. Mrs. Goldbloom and I helped her to the car as people on the street looked on.

"This is Mackenzie," I said. "Thanks for helping."

Mrs. Goldbloom gave me a soft but worried smile. At the hospital, she said she'd watch Ozzie for us. I guess there were a few Good Samaritans left after all.

In the emergency department, Mac was checked over and cleaned up.

The doctor asked me to go, but I said I wouldn't leave her side and so was allowed to stay. The doctor didn't like it, but he didn't push it. Mackenzie was complaining of a pain in her chest, and an X-ray was taken. It showed she had a cracked rib, but there was nothing they could do except give her pain medication. The doctor said, "You should spend the night in the hospital."

"No," Mackenzie insisted. "I want to go home." It seemed odd that she had used that word again.

"First you'll have to meet with a social worker. Maybe you'll need to file a police report too. Stay here."

When he walked away, Mac looked at the door. "We gotta leave. Now."

"Are you sure?"

"Yes."

I held her hand, and we got up and walked out of the examining room. The waiting room was filled with hurt and sick people, so no one seemed to notice us as we walked down the hall and out the door.

"What happened today?" I asked. "Who was that guy?"

"I can't talk about it," she said. "I just can't." And now it began to sink in. I knew what Mackenzie had been doing these last few weeks. I knew what she'd done to bail out Ozzie and to get enough money for us to stay at Eddy's. I shuddered. I squeezed her hand tightly.

Outside, Mrs. Goldbloom was walking Ozzie on the grass. She saw us and came over, deep concern on her face.

"Are you all right?" she asked Mac.

"Yes," Mac said. "Can you give us a ride?"

"Of course," she answered. "Where to?"

Neither of us had an answer.

## Chapter Seventeen

As Mrs. Goldbloom drove on, an awkward silence came over Mackenzie and me. She looked frightened, and when I touched her, she pulled away. "I'm sorry I got you into this," she said.

"You didn't get me into anything. You helped me out when I was kicked out of my house."

"I think I just want to go somewhere. Somewhere far, far away." She was looking out the window, and I could feel that I was losing her.

She tapped Mrs. Goldbloom on the shoulder. "Can you pull over? I think I just want to get out here."

Mrs. Goldbloom slowed the car.

"No," I said. "Don't stop."

But she had already pulled over. Mac started to open the door, and I grabbed her. She winced from the pain. "Don't go," I said. "I won't let you." I could see she was determined to bolt. "Please," I said. "Stay with me."

Mrs. Goldbloom turned to her. "He's right. Don't go. I have someone I want you to meet."

Mackenzie was in pain, and I wondered if we had made a mistake leaving the hospital. She slumped back in her seat. She still wouldn't let me hold her hand. Whatever was about to happen, I was sure I was losing her. And that scared the hell out of me. I didn't want to be alone.

Mrs. Goldbloom pulled back into the traffic. Soon we were at the north end of town. She stopped in front of a big old Victorian house with fading paint. "This is where my friend lives," she said. "You'll like her."

Inside the house, in a long cold hallway, Mrs. Goldbloom introduced us to a large stern woman. "This is Margaret Sampson," she said.

Margaret didn't give a good first impression. She looked at Mackenzie, studied her. Then she scowled at me as if I was the one who had beat her up. She looked at Ozzie and shook her head.

"You two have names?"

"I'm Cam. This is Mac."

"And the mutt?"

"Ozzie."

Margaret looked at Mrs. Goldbloom. "We're full, Ruth. We can't take in anyone else. And we don't take dogs. You know that." I didn't know what she was talking about.

Mrs. Goldbloom smiled at Margaret, and the two of them just looked at each other for an awkward and long few seconds. Then Margaret sighed. "Let's go inside, shall we?" she said.

In the living room, a bunch of kids were lounging around, some doing what looked like schoolwork, some just chatting. I thought I recognized a face or two from school. They watched as we walked past them and into the kitchen. A couple of girls petted Ozzie along the way.

It wasn't an ordinary kitchen. It was more like the cafeteria kitchen, only smaller. We sat down at a wooden table. "You can see we already have a crowd," Margaret said.

Mackenzie looked really uncomfortable, and I could tell she didn't like this Margaret Sampson at all. "I'm not sure what's going on here," I said. "We didn't ask to come here."

Margaret made a face and looked at Mrs. Goldbloom, who turned to Mac and me and began to explain. "Margaret is a retired social worker. She quit her job because she saw the system was failing so many kids. She opened her home to some of them. She doesn't get any government funding, so she has to fund-raise. I help her with that sometimes."

"It's been a bit rough this year," Margaret now added. She'd lost a bit of the edge in her voice. "What with the economy and all." She was looking at Mac, but Mac had moved off into her own world. Margaret looked back at me. I held her gaze. I could see there was more to this woman than I'd first thought. It was like she could read my mind, conjure our story. She knew we had no place else to go.

"We have rules here," she said suddenly. "Lots of rules." She handed me a sheet of paper. She was right. There were a lot of rules. Strict ones. Old-fashioned rules. "Not everyone can live by them."

As I studied them, I began to see some hope.

"You two in school?" she asked.

"Yes," I said.

"Good." She studied Mackenzie some more. "She been to a doctor?" she asked me.

"Yes," I said.

"If you want to keep the dog, you'll have to sleep in the basement. It's not pretty, but it's warm and dry. You'll have to fix it up yourself. But there are no guarantees. We might lose this place tomorrow. Anything can happen."

"I understand," I said.

"And the rules?"

"We're good with the rules," I said.

"You two talk it over, make sure it's what you both want to do," Margaret said, and then she and Mrs. Goldbloom left the kitchen.

Mac was crying now and leaning into me. "I don't know if I can do this," she said.

"*We* can do this," I said. "Together."

"I'm not sure I even understand what kind of place this is. Where are we?"

"We're home," I said. "We're finally home."

Lesley Choyce is the author of eighty-four books for adults, teens and kids. He runs Pottersfield Press, teaches at Dalhousie University and lives at Lawrencetown Beach, Nova Scotia, where he surfs year-round. A recent book, *I'm Alive, I Believe in Everything*, is a collection of his poems written over forty years and was short-listed for the Atlantic Poetry Prize. His website is www.lesleychoyce.com.